CHRISTMAS KISSES

A TWISTED CHRISTMAS SHORT STORY

ALEXANDRIA BLAELOCK

BlueMere Books
MELBOURNE, AUSTRALIA

BlueMere Books
www.bluemerebooks.com

CHISTMAS KISSES

va Gibson walked across the green marble foyer floor, refusing to look any higher than the floor.

When she reached the edge of the stairs down onto the ballroom floor, she paused, closing her eyes to fully soak up the atmosphere.

The room was more or less silent, with the hum of quiet conversation amongst those decorating the last of the tables.

She heard the odd chink of crockery and cutlery as the last of the covers were laid out.

Clashes as crates of glasses were stacked up out ready to be filled and passed around by tuxedo clad waiters.

The band tuned their guitars and checked the sound.

The room seemed a little warm, but she'd been running around most of the day getting everything organised and set up.

A cool breeze drifted across her tank top clad shoulders as the air-conditioning cranked up a notch, preparing for the influx of hundreds of dinner guests.

The hotel was too posh to let any cooking smells into the function rooms, but just for a moment, she thought perhaps she could smell the perfume of roasting meats.

After a few more seconds savouring the moment, she pointed her face up, out across the room and opened her eyes.

It looked magnificent.

Even if she did say it herself.

Traditional Christmas with an Australian twist.

Huge garlands of red flowering gum twined with strings of fairy lights and white, silver and gold glass baubles were suspended from the ceiling. They criss-crossed the room, and where they met, gold and silver stars hung, swaying slightly in the strengthening air-conditioning.

Bouquets of gum leaves were mixed with gold and silver painted pine cones were tied up string and hung at intervals along the balustrades of the sweeping stair case.

Large round tables for ten surrounded the edges of the rich, dark red wood parquetry dance floor.

They were spread with thick white tablecloths, the place settings marked with a red plate, topped with a white Christmas themed plate and a starched red napkin folded into a swan.

In the centre of each table, a silver platter held a small, brown paper covered pot tied up with hessian string containing a small, decorated Christmas tree.

No candles unfortunately; health and safety wouldn't allow them.

The stage at the rear held a square steel lighting stand, decorated with garlands of large red, green and gold ribbons, also twined with twinkling lights. A large wreath of the same materials was suspended from the top of the frame.

The band left the stage to wait for the first set, and the room's internal PA system started playing the Christmas songs.

It was just perfect.

Goldings Investment Bank was the biggest bank in Melbourne, and if they liked what she'd done, it might even make her reputation.

She let out the breath she hadn't realised she was holding, and started to critically assess each part of the room.

Goldings could just as easily ruin her reputation as make it. Her event management business wasn't established enough to take any of it for granted.

But.

It all looked to be in order.

Ava checked her watch, and decided she just had enough time for a quick shower before she changed into her evening gown and came back to oversee the operation of the evening.

She hadn't seen her boyfriend Max by the time she left the room, though that wasn't really unusual. He was busy with his software start-up, and she rarely saw him these days.

The plan was to spend a few days over the Christmas break at his family home by the sea in Portland, and as long as he was at the hotel in the morning, that was fine.

She came from an outer-east Melbourne suburb nestled in the Dandenong Ranges, and found his beachside home and fishing family lifestyle utterly charming despite his complaints.

His dinner ticket, and the hotel room, were complimentary. He wouldn't know anyone at the Goldings Christmas Dinner, and she'd be working, so he probably wouldn't enjoy himself anyway.

But maybe they could get to know each other again while they were away. Rekindle their tired romance.

And if they couldn't, then maybe it was just time to move on.

After all, ten years after uni, they were very different people to the ones who'd met then.

But that was a problem for another day - she didn't have time to worry about the state of her relationship right at that moment.

Guests were starting to assemble as she slipped back into the room and made her way to the rear.

She could not help but notice the blonde man in the tailored dinner suit - he was literally head and shoulders above everyone else in the room.

Besides, his hair was curling around his collar, and it was so rare to see a curly headed man.

As her gaze lingered on his surfer sleek body, he must have felt it and turned around to look in her direction.

She quickly ducked and pretended to adjust her silver heeled Mary Janes. Amazingly comfortable *and* bought on sale.

But when she stood up again, he was still looking at her, with a gaze so dark and intense she had to hold a nearby chair for support.

And as she went through the remainder of the preparations for the dinner, she could feel him looking at her.

Every time she saw him from the corner of her eye, she couldn't help but turn to look, and she would see him looking back at her and once more avoid his gaze.

And every single time, she felt her heart flutter and her body flush.

It was clear she couldn't afford to get entangled with him. He was either the kind of man who didn't extend the first night to the second day, or the kind of man who demanded nothing short of surrender.

Either way, he was bad news, and threatened her hard won independence.

In her calculations, she completely forgot to factor in Max.

Ryan Griffith paused at the top of the stairs to look at the decorated room.

But not for long; he wasn't a Christmassy kind of guy.

The thing that did make him pause was the woman - he couldn't help but notice the woman.

For a start, she was wearing a very modest red dress. Longish sleeves, high neckline, and a long, wide skirt that clung to her legs without petticoats.

In a sea of tight, revealing, black dresses, you'd have to be blind not to notice her.

For a second, she'd bent over to do something to her shoe. A feat of some athleticism to bend from the waist, reaching the shoe without crouching.

She looked like a vintage ad for stockings, bent forward into an exceedingly pleasing R shape.

For a third, when she finally stood, cheeks slightly flushed, and shook her golden hair out, she looked like a fully clothed Botticelli's Venus. Would she be as lush as the painting underneath her dress?

He pulled himself together.

She looked like Christmas personified.

Then lost it again, thinking he was fully prepared to be her Santa any time she chose…

He shut his mouth with a snap.

Who, exactly, was she?

Not someone from Goldings, he was fairly sure he'd have noticed her; every beautiful woman in the place had approached him, and there were precious few whose outer beautify matched their inner.

Certainly no one he'd consider more than a couple of hours with, and he had a feeling his mystery woman was a keeper.

He descended the stairs, walked to the bar, and ordered a Whiskey Sour, swirling it absently in the glass as he watched her move around the room.

She didn't stop to speak with any of the assembled guests, just stood aside a little and waited for them to move on.

All the while scanning the crowd, perhaps looking for her date.

And then she stopped and spoke with a waiter, who indicated a hidden door through which she disappeared.

Not looking for her boyfriend then, but something to do with the event, perhaps managing it.

Someone from the hotel then.

Surely his mate Seth would've mentioned someone as gorgeous as that working here.

He sipped his drink, and waited for the woman to return. Chatting easily with his colleagues as they waited for drinks, but not encouraging anyone to linger.

The level in his drink glass gradually dropped, but she hadn't returned by the time the Master of Ceremonies had ascended the stage and invited the guests to be seated for the first course.

He strolled to the notice board, right of the bar, located his allocated table, and then found it.

Near the back, enticingly close to that hidden door.

But probably not close enough to be the recipient of any awards.

Not to worry, he hadn't planned to stay for the whole night anyway. Just to make an appearance, eat some of the extortionately priced dinner, and then leave.

He wouldn't have come at all, except he was obliged. These kind of events weren't really his thing.

As the table filled up, he traded inconsequentialities with his colleagues, until there were two seats left.

To his left.

With no name plates.

As the Master of Ceremonies started his patter, waiters circulated with glasses of champagne.

Welcome to the Goldings Annual Christmas Dinner. Evacuation exits here, here and here. Assembly areas there, there and there. Please welcome the band. The evening's agenda. The giving of Awards, and so on.

Ryan had heard it all so many times before he barely listened, just tilted his wrist to check the time and calculate how much longer before he could leave.

And then, in a cloud of sweet, floral perfume, the woman in the red dress sat next to him and laid a small red bag on the table.

Seeming not to notice the empty seat, she nodded politely to him, the man on her left, and the rest of table.

For a moment he was struck dumb, couldn't think of a single thing to say to her, and it filled him with dread.

Was he losing his touch?

Or possibly worse, was he that worried about making a hash of it?

The table stood to toast the successful year and the hope of the same for the new year.

He struggled to pull himself together and get his feet underneath him.

Telling himself to be cool.

As they sat again, she leaned slightly toward him, and thinking she wanted to talk, he leaned across to see what she had to say and their heads cracked together as they sat down.

Loud enough to make their dinner companions look to see the source of the sound.

She made a small sound of pain and put her hand up to touch her head, miscalculated the distance, and landed a blow to his jaw.

She made another small sound of pain.

He leaned away from her and rubbed his jaw, "that's quite a punch you have there!"

Her earnest brown eyes checked to see he was okay, "I'm so sorry, are you all right?"

"Yeah, I'm fine."

"Just as well," some wag across the table said, "wouldn't want to see you making an OHS claim this early in the evening."

Ryan glared across the table, unable to identify the speaker. Turning back to the woman, he asked, "what about you, are you okay?"

"Fine," she dropped her hand from her head, and turned the palm to face him, "see, no blood. It's all good.

"Wait," she said, her face shading towards white. She reached for her napkin, wrapping it around her hand, and holding it tight, "I think I caught your tooth on the way."

"I'll get some help," Ryan glanced around, looking for a waiter or someone else to call over for assistance, and when he turned back to her, she was half out of her chair.

"I'll just pop out the back and find the first aider. I know more or less where the kit should be."

As she cleared her chair, she stumbled as she caught the toe of her shoe in the hem of her skirt.

Ryan leapt up to help her, but she left him behind and almost sprinted across the small gap to disappear through the hidden door.

He looked around again, saw no one coming to help, but one or two guests looking curiously at him.

I'll just go make sure she's okay," he said, and scooping up her small bag, followed her through the door.

"Shit, shit, shit," Ava chanted as she trotted down the brightly lit service corridor towards the Conference Manager's office.

Not so much because she was injured, though she felt like her hand was on fire, but because she felt like she'd made a fool of herself.

A big fool.

The biggest fool.

She risked opening the napkin to look at her index finger and the back of her hand.

Still bleeding. She really hoped it didn't need stitches.

But it definitely needed a dressing of some kind.

Fortunately, the Night Event Manager, Seth, had given her a quick safety and security run down, so she knew he was the First Aider.

Luckily, he was in his office, so she didn't have to go looking for him or someone else to open the locked First Aid cabinet.

He rinsed the wound down with some saline, "looks nasty, what did you cut it on?"

"My chipped tooth," said someone behind her. She recognised the smell of his soap, and glanced over her shoulder to see the gorgeous man who'd cracked her head.

The Night Manager laughed, "I told you to go see a dentist Ryan," he said, then selected a couple of dressings from the kit.

He glanced up at her as he arranged the first one down her finger, "Ava have you met Ryan Griffith?"

She shook her head.

"Pleased to meet you," he said.

She smiled faintly and nodded her head, she had no plans to see him again.

Ever.

"Ava Gibson here's the Event Manager who organised Golding's Christmas Dinner," he told Ryan.

"You've done a good job."

Ava winced as Seth applied the second dressing around the edge of her hand.

"Sorry," Seth said. "this's partly my fault. I chipped his tooth at squash last week."

Ava attempted to smile through her gritted teeth, "you know each other then?" as if she cared about the answer.

"Best mates since high school," he wound a bandage around her hand and wrist to secure the dressing.

She grunted. It had hurt before, but after cleaning it, dressing it, and now compressing it, her hand was almost unbearably painful.

"There's quite a lot of blood, so you're probably going to need stitches. I've bound it fairly tightly, but I think you should go to the emergency room to get it looked at properly."

"I'll take you," said Ryan.

"Nonsense," she said, standing up, "I'm here to do a job, and I'm going to see it through."

A wave of dizziness hit her, and she sat down abruptly.

Ryan leapt across the room to steady her, and his hands burned like fire through the thin silk of her gown.

"Maybe I'll just go back to my room to lie down for a little while."

Seth put his palm across her forehead, "You're a bit warm, I really think you should go to hospital, but I can't force you."

"Perhaps tomorrow, if I still feel bad."

She stood, holding the back of the chair for support.

Seth shuffled some folders on his desk, picked one and quickly skimmed the contents. "Your notes are clear and concise, and now that food service's begun, there's nothing of great significance to be done, so don't be fretting about the rest of the party."

She nodded, winced and touched her head.

"Let me see you back to your room," Ryan said.

All Ava wanted to do was get to her room, but Seth clapped Ryan's shoulder, "good man, make sure she's okay."

And to Ava, "do you want me to get some soup or something sent to your room?"

"No thanks. I just want to go lie down. Thanks Seth."

Seth nodded, "try to keep the bandage elevated."

Ryan slipped an arm around her shoulders. Standing next to him, she realised he was even more ridiculously tall than she'd thought.

Romances would call her petite, or some such nonsense, but compared to him, she was a dwarf.

Bashful most likely.

And not entirely sure that his proximity wasn't the entire reason she felt dizzy rather than a knock on the head in conjunction with the hand trauma.

Compared to Max, he was tall *and* strong.

She was the strong one in their relationship - any jars that needed opening, she opened them. Spiders that needed removing from the bath, also her. Not to mention putting the bins out.

Or just bloody going out and earning a living.

Just for a moment, she allowed herself to snuggle into the warmth under his shoulder.

To lean on him, letting herself imagine he would take care of her.

To place her wounded hand alongside his heart, imagining she could feel it beat, slowly and steadily beneath her fingers.

All too soon, they arrived at her room.

"Key?" he asked.

She fished it out of her bag and gave it to him, smothering a small smile at the notional chivalry of the gesture.

He insert it in the digital lock, she heard it click.

He paused, lowered door handle in his hand.

He was taking too long, so she leaned around him and pushed the door with her left hand.

She took him by surprise, and he fell in through the door.

He hooked an arm around her waist and swung her against his chest as he turned his back to the room.

"What the hell do you think you're doing?" she demanded.

And only then did she hear the voice of a woman, "Max, don't stop, I'm nearly there."

She tried to look around Ryan's body, but he held her firm. She looked up at him and he shook his head.

Ava forced his arms open and his body out of her way, and watched her boyfriend try to disentangle himself from some red-headed woman.

She heard ringing in her ears and felt a sharp pain in her head. She struggled to put her hand to her head, took a step, and watched the floor rise up to meet her.

《《 • 》》

Ryan panicked as she fell over, but managed to grab a hold of her before she hit the floor.

He watched the man try to disentangle himself from the woman for a moment, then opened the door and supported Ava through it.

Letting the door close, he shrugged her into a more comfortable position, cradling her in his arms.

He strode back down the corridor, fighting off a red haze of fury.

With whichever one of those people was Ava's partner. Hell, both of them!

With Seth for not ensuring she went to hospital.

And with himself for not stopping her from seeing what was going on in the room.

He pushed the button for a lift, and thankfully, the carriage was waiting where they'd left it.

As the doors slid closed, the man from Ava's room, still trying to get his pants on was trying to run down the corridor.

"Wait! Who are you? What are you doing with my girlfriend."

Max then.

Bloody check of him calling Ava his girlfriend given what he'd just been doing.

With *another* woman.

Coming out on the ground floor, he went straight for the taxi rank rather than calling a valet to get his car.

He didn't want her so called boyfriend finding her before she'd had a chance to think in peace.

And to get the appropriate treatment.

That slimy bastard boyfriend probably had some kind of pathetic excuse.

"Royal Melbourne Hospital," he said as he stowed her safely in the back seat and climbed in beside her. He fastened her seatbelt as the cab pulled away.

"What happened?" the driver asked.

"Cut her hand and hit her head. Concussion I think."

The driver indicated, "should've called an ambulance mate," he said as he paused waiting for the traffic to clear.

"No time. Probably quicker this way anyway."

The driver nodded, and sped up the car a little, weaving in and around the traffic.

Before too long, the were pulling up outside the hospital.

Ryan threw a bunch of twenties at the driver, "keep the change," he said as he released the seatbelt and slid her out.

"She's lucky to have a guy like you," the driver said, toasting him with the cash, "good luck mate."

Ryan nodded, and carried her into the emergency department.

Unfortunately, being Friday night, the place was packed.

The noise of drunk or drugged young men screaming was deafening, and the chaos was almost enough to make him back away and take her somewhere else.

There were no seats available, even if he'd been prepared to leave her unattended.

Ava weighed barely more than a mouse, so for the moment at least, he was content to hold her in his arms.

Happily, a nurse approached him, and after hearing what had happened, brought him through to a large, cool, air-conditioned ward and invited him to lay Ava on a bed.

"We'll need to get her gown off," he said, "are you comfortable taking care of that?"

Ryan blushed, and stuttered something, and the nurse laughed.

"I'll get one of my female colleagues to take care of it."

A short while later a female nurse ushered him out, and a short while after that, he was invited back into the cubicle.

Ava was tucked into a hospital gown and the blanket drawn up to her waist.

Her dress was neatly folded on the chair along with her shoes and stockings.

The nurse checked her temperature, blood pressure and pulse, flashed a torch in her eyes, and started filling out the admission forms.

Not that Ryan was able to help with much of them - name, but no medical history, Medicare details or contact details.

"I'm happy to go guarantor until you can speak with her," he said.

She nodded, "Doctor will be with you shortly," she said as she drew the curtains around the sides of the bed.

Ryan looked around at the grubby ward, the bustling staff, and didn't know what to do with himself.

He took his tie off and tucked it into his jacket pocket, then packed her dress and shoes inside his jacket like a gift, and held it in his lap as he dropped into the chair next to her bed.

"Hang in there kiddo," he said, taking her hand.

It seemed like forever before a doctor came to see them, pushing a mobile steel cabinet with drawers before her.

She checked Ava's chart as she introduced herself, "I'm Doctor Stephenson, can you tell me what happened?"

Ryan quickly related the events of the evening, as the young woman rinsed her hands in an alcohol solution and slipped on some gloves.

She unwrapped the bandage from Ava's right hand, and dropped it in a medical waste bag hanging off the back of the cabinet.

Putting on her safety glasses she examined the wound, "your First Aider's done a good job, but it definitely needs stitches."

She put a disposable towel on a tray on top of the cabinet, pulled a bunch of dressings together on the tray along with a threaded needle.

She injected a local anaesthetic, and dropped the syringe in the sharps bin at the other end of the cabinet.

Then cleaned the cut again, and put in five stitches.

As she moved onto dressing and bandaging the wound, Ryan said, "Look, I don't actually know her, but she's just finished managing a major event so I'd wager she's not been eating or sleeping as well as she could've been."

The doctor glanced at him, frowned, and then nodded.

She added a cannula to the tray then inserted it into the back of Ava's left hand. "I'll order some blood tests to check her levels, and I'll administer some antibiotics via a drip."

She finished dressing the wound, winding the bandage around the hand and partway up her arm, when he was done she placed it on Ava's chest.

"Try to keep her hand elevated above the heart as long as you can, and you can take the bandage off tomorrow."

Ryan nodded.

She folded the towel like an envelope over the packaging left on the tray and dropped it in the bin. Then wrote a bunch of stuff on the chart.

"It's all good," she said stripping off her gloves and tossing them in the bin. "We'll keep her here for an hour or two, and then decide whether to transfer her to a ward or release her. The nurse will be back in a moment with the drip."

She left the cubicle, and moved onto the next.

For the moment at least, he and Ava were more or less alone.

Aside from the beeping machines, the moans of other patients, and the quite hum of conversation.

He closed his eyes, rested his head on Ava's legs, and listened to the late night sound of the emergency department.

He found himself silently chanting, "please be okay. Please be okay. Please be okay."

A nurse woke him by bustling into the cubicle. He quickly connected up the drip, then injected the antibiotics into it.

"No response yet?"

"Not yet."

He applied a tourniquet, drew blood, and released the constriction.

"I shouldn't worry, it's still fairly early."

Ryan nodded.

Surprised by the strength of his desire to protect her.

Not just from the fallout of her traumatic injury, but from her boyfriend's infidelity as well.

Once more he laid his forehead on her legs, and willed her to wake up and get better.

《《 • 》》

When Ava woke, she was surprised to be in a hospital ward with off-white by grey walls and floor.

Even more surprised to be dressed in a hospital gown.

She panicked, plucked at the bed covers to pull them higher, and noticed the cannula in her hand.

Then she saw her dress, on a hanger, hanging on the inside of the curtain rail where she could see it, and relaxed.

Ahead of her there was a gap in the curtains through which she could see red and purple streaked skies though a large window, and assumed it was dawn the next day.

Quiet conversation came from outside the room, and the sound of soft snoring from within.

Her hand was warm and snug in a man's grasp, "Max," she croaked quietly.

And then she realised the hair was blonde and curly, not straight and mouse-brown.

His white shirt was open at the neck, and he'd rolled up his sleeves.

She glanced around to see his jacket was slung over the back of the hospital chair, and he'd tucked his bow tie in the pocket.

From her vantage point it looked to be a tie-it-yourself bow tie rather than the ready-made kind.

She smiled, remembering how she used to tie them for her father, and being disappointed that Max found them too complicated and preferred ready-made.

Even though they never sat quite right on him.

Then again, she'd already checked out the tailoring of his potentially bespoke suit.

A little larger in the shoulders, arms and legs to accommodate his muscles. And a little trimmer in the waist and hips to form a pleasingly triangular silhouette.

As her brain ticked through the differences, she realised he was Ryan Griffith - the man she'd been attracted too from the Golding's dinner.

She felt a little curl of heat within her as she contemplated her relative lack of clothing protection.

Ava wanted to pull her hand away, but at the same time, she wanted to hold it tightly and never let it go.

Max had been all the future she'd imagined.

He was her first major crush, and she'd been so overcome by love for him, she'd lost all interest in any kind of career or education.

Romanticising caring for his home and kids, she'd withdrawn from Uni to take care of him.

Never once broadened her thinking to wonder whether she, herself, was happy with that.

And recalling what she'd seen the night before, he'd probably never thought seriously about her future either.

It was the harshest of possible lessons, and she wondered if she could get past that.

Wondered if she could forgive him.

Pick up where she'd left off, visit his parents for Christmas, stay with him and forget that she'd caught him *in flagrante*.

Mind you, if she'd caught him once, how often had he been with other women while they were supposed to be together?

And was it something he would keep doing?

Most likely.

Just not in her work-related hotel room.

She grimaced – he had such poor judgement.

So much wiser to go somewhere else and not risk getting caught.

Did he think she was so stupid she wouldn't notice the rumpled sheets or the smell of another woman's perfume?

Though maybe she already had, countless times after a long hard day at work.

Was it time to think about moving on without Max in her life?

She turned her focus towards Ryan Griffith.

She'd met him less than twenty-four hours ago, and he was currently asleep on her leg, clutching her hand in his.

Perhaps he wasn't the playboy she had assumed.

Gippsland dairy farm boy made good?
From running around after cows to running around share trading and floating companies at Goldings?

Or did he have an overdeveloped sense of duty.

Despite her experience with Max, she couldn't stop herself from imagining a golden future with Ryan Griffith.

Early morning trips to Sorrento beach to go surfing. Cruising the lanes for cocktails. Antiquing in Tyabb.

His naked body entwined with hers.

And later, lithe beautiful children, blonde haired and sun bronzed who looked just like him.

Adorable.

Now that she was fully awake, she needed a drink of water.

And the bathroom.

Not necessarily in that order.

She looked around and over her shoulders to find out where the drip was, and of course it was attached to the bed.

Turning around to look at Ryan to gauge the possibility of moving him, she noticed one eye was open, and it was looking at her.

She blushed.

He smiled a lazy, half-asleep smile, "mornin."

"I need some help with the bathroom."

And then it was his turn to blush, and she laughed.

"Not using it, just getting the drip down so I can go."

"Not that I wouldn't if you needed me to," he said, getting up to pull it down, " but I'm relieved you don't."

He held the bag for her, and held out a hand to steady her as she approached the edge of the bed and eased off it onto the floor.

Then he walked with her to the bathroom tucked into the corner of the room, and waited outside while she used it.

When she was done, she washed her hands and couldn't help noticing she looked a fright. Even without the drip bag between her teeth.

"You look like the Wreck of the Hesperus," she told herself as she tried to finger-comb her hair into some kind of order.

Then gave it up as a bad job and settled for rinsing her mouth and splashing her face with water.

She glanced doubtfully in the mirror again, and wasn't entirely sure she'd improved the situation.

Still, he'd seen her worse.

One last go at her hair, and she reminded herself he'd seen her better too.

«« • »»

Ryan had watched her sleep, on and off throughout the night.

Trying to think of a way to keep her with him longer.

Could he invite her for breakfast? Maybe she'd find the hospital breakfast to her liking.

And even if she didn't, where could he take her? Was inviting her to his apartment too forward?

He knocked on the bathroom door, "are you okay in there."

A muffled reply came from within, which he took as reassurance she was okay.

A short time later, she came out, and he took the drip back from her, fixing it back to the bed as she hopped into it.

"What's the time?"

He checked his watch, "six am."

"You know, I didn't get anything to eat last night, and I'm absolutely starving."

"I can go down to the ground floor café and get you something if you like."

"Do you think they'd have a bacon sandwich?"

He shrugged.

"Maybe a toasted ham, cheese and tomato sandwich then; I can pay you back okay?"

"I think I can spring you a toasted sandwich seeing as I almost killed you."

She snorted, "you did not."

"I dunno, it was touch and go for a while there."

She sobered instantly, "was it?"

He nudged her shoulder, "hey, I'm kidding!"

She put her uninjured hand on her chest, "you had me going for a while there."

"Clearly you need some food - would you prefer tea or coffee?"

"Latte please, no sugar."

"Then I shall fetch your order forthwith," he bowed ostentatiously.

Grabbing his wallet from his jacket, he saluted her and left the room.

Filled with a sudden burst of energy, he took the stairs, jumping down two at a time.

And as he reached the café, he caught the smell of frying bacon, and smiled. He ordered the toasted sandwich, a bacon sandwich, and two of the biggest size lattes.

The café was packed with people in scrubs, so his order took a little while, and he fretted about Ava as he paced up and down the length of the counter.

And when it was done, and packed into a carry bag, he stuffed a bunch of sauce sachets in too, and walked back up the stairs.

She was sitting up when he got back.

Someone had moved the table across the bed, and gotten her a water jug, a cup of something he supposed might have been coffee, and a couple of packets of biscuits.

"I have hunted," he said as he walked through the door, "and I have returned victorious."

She laughed, and the sound was so bright and cheerful and alive, he wanted to hear more of it.

"So," he said as he unpacked, "I got both sandwiches, so you can take your pick."

She made a grab for the latte and took a long drink of coffee, before she answered, smacking her lips and saying, "aahhh, I needed that.

"You must be hungry too, why don't we both have half of each?"

"Oh. I hadn't thought about it, but I just realised I am."

It might have seemed obvious to her, but Ryan thought it was kind.

He wracked his brain trying to think of the last time someone had been spontaneously kind to him.

And that was actually impossible; investment banking wasn't the kind of field that generally attracted kind people.

She picked up one wrapped packet and handed the other to him, tearing open the layers of papers to reveal the sandwich. "Bacon," she said, "is there any brown sauce?"

He shuffled through the sauce packets, "tomato... or... barbecue."

He watched, faintly horrified and disgusted as she reached for the barbecue, lifted the top slice of bread and squirted it over the bacon.

"It's really nice! Really. Do you want to try it?" she held the sandwich out to him.

He made a face, but leaned over and took a bite, chewing slowly and cautiously, but she was right.

It was tasty.

He grunted and nodded his head, "not sure I'll be giving up tomato sauce just yet."

He sipped some coffee, then unwrapped the toasted ham, cheese and tomato. Moaning a little as he enjoyed the first bite.

They enjoyed their coffee and the rest of the sandwiches in a companionable silence.

Ava was kind of relaxing to be around.

No demands for attention or feats of indulgence.

Nor did she insist of filling the air with the sound of her voice, for the sake of hearing it.

He wondered whether her boyfriend was the drama queen in that relationship, and once more felt a wave of anger that he was taking the gorgeous woman sitting in front of him for granted.

"Any idea when I can get out of here?" she asked.

"What? No.

"Sorry, when they moved you to the ward, the doctor said they'll assess you this morning, and then decide."

"Ah," she wiped her hands on a napkin. "And why did they decide to admit me?"

"You were dehydrated, and something about levels, and something about the stitches."

She raised one eyebrow, and he loved her for it.

He shrugged, "I didn't understand three-quarters of it. I'm just glad they didn't accuse me of giving you tetanus!"

She laughed again.

Not long after they'd finished eating, the doctor and a gaggle of students came to check Ava, and he was banished until they'd completed the check.

As the doctor left, he told Ryan, "the bandage can come off this morning, and we'll put some dressings on, but don't let them get wet. For pain relief, a couple of paracetamol tablets four hourly, or as needed."

He nodded and the flock moved on.

Ava rolled her eyes at him as he entered the room.

"Typical telling the guy what needs to be done. Now we just have to wait for the nurse to take care of the bandages and we can go," she said.

《《 • 》》

Almost as soon as the words were out of her mouth, Ava winced.

Much as she liked the idea of him sticking around, she had no right to assume he would.

He wasn't her boyfriend.

And then she remembered what she'd seen the night before again. And where exactly was the cheater?

"Where's Max?" she asked.

His face reddened as he sat on the edge of the chair.

He averted his eyes, and picked at a fingernail. "He aah, well I...

"Look I'm sorry to be crude, and maybe overstepping your boundaries, but he was shagging some girl, and I didn't want him here with you begging for forgiveness, or telling you it was a mistake, or he never meant to hurt you, or whatever. I didn't want him stressing you out and distracting you from getting the care you needed."

It *was* kind of high-handed, but Max would have done exactly what Ryan thought he might.

By the time she left hospital, he would probably have talked her around, and she would have gone with him out of habit.

And when, for that matter, had Max last shagged *her*?

She sighed.

"So I saw what I thought I saw."

"Yes."

"And did you..." she waved up at the dress.

His colour had been returning to normal, but he blushed again, "oh no. Oh god no. One of the nurses took care of that."

She laughed at his embarrassment, and couldn't resist teasing him, "so you wouldn't want too..."

He sucked in his breath, and looked at her, "I didn't say that. I just said that at this time, in this particular location, I didn't undress you."

It was the oddest thing, she'd thought his eyes were bright blue, but as she looked into their depths, she realised they were a more of a deep teal colour.

He leaned towards her, looked searchingly into her eyes, "trust me, when the right time comes, I won't hesitate to take your clothes off one by one."

She wasn't really aware that she'd leaned closer towards him.

But thankfully, or maybe not, a nurse chose that moment to walk in, "I'm here to take out the... Oh, do you guys want me to come back later."

Ryan leaned back with, was that disappointment on his face?

Ava knew she was disappointed, though what she'd hoped might happen was another thing.

Quite possibly best not pursued in a shared hospital ward.

She sat back, "no. I'm more than ready to get out of here."

"I bet you are," the nurse said with a wink, "I'll try to be as quick as I can. I'll take care of the drip first, then check the wound."

And to Ryan, "if you'd excuse us please?" She waited until he'd left the room.

Ava looked at the door, and wished he'd stayed behind.

What the hell was it going to be like to let him go.

The nurse clamped off the drip, removed it from the cannula, and pulled the tape loose.

She picked up a cotton wool ball, held it in place, then pulled the attachment out. "Put some pressure on this will you?" she asked as she disposed of the drip and cannula.

Then she checked it, "all good," and put a tiny padded sticker on the insertion point.

"Now let's check the stitches." She unwound the bandage, found there was no blood, either on it or the dressings beneath.

"I just need to make sure there's no signs of infection in the wound," she said, gently removing the dressings and nodding. "Nice and neat," she said approvingly, taping it up with another dressing.

She told Ava how to care for it, and as she left the room, she heard her telling Ryan how to take care of it too.

She smiled ruefully at him as he re-entered the room, and he winked at her.

"Another pair of ears is always good," he said, "so you can leave now?"

She swallowed the sudden lump in her throat.

Clearly she'd got the wrong idea, and he wanted to be rid of her.

Now she had to think of what to do with her day - she couldn't go home, and she couldn't go back to the hotel.

And without doing either of those things, she had nothing aside from her dinner gown and high heels to wear.

She couldn't go anywhere without people looking at her, and assuming she'd been out all night with some guy.

And while she had, it wasn't the kind of out with a guy that anyone would be imagining.

She couldn't buy anything, because she didn't have any cash or a credit card, as she'd planned on staying in the function hotel.

God it was a nightmare, but better to get the pain over before it got any worse.

"Yes. Don't feel obliged to stay, I can manage."

Damn it, her lip quivered and her eyes filled with tears. She swallowed again, and closed her eyes.

And felt a tear ease out of her closed lids and turned away.

He sat on the edge of the bed, and smoothed the tear away with the pad of his thumb.

"I don't want to leave you like this," he said.

"So. Um... Um... I...

"Would you like to go out for lunch with me?"

She smiled, because as it turned out, he did want to spend time with her.

And also because it didn't seem to matter to him whether or not he looked or sounded like an idiot with her.

At least not at that moment.

She so wanted to kiss him right then.

Instead, she said, "why don't you step outside and I'll get dressed."

He grinned, "I'm looking forward to seeing you again," and stepped out.

Ava did a little dance, then pulled off the hospital gown, pulled her dress off its hanger, and hurriedly got dressed.

She didn't want to waste any time. Or risk him leaving without her.

《《 • 》》

Ryan ducked out of the room, and did a little happy dance of his own.

He couldn't believe he'd almost let her blow him off like that.

If he hadn't seen that tear, he would've left, assuming she didn't want to see him.

It didn't bear thinking about.

He put his hand over his heart and tried to imagine how awful that Ava shaped hole would be.

They'd barely spoken to each other, yet... he couldn't imagine a life without her in it.

The comfortable silences, the feel of her perfect fit under his arm, and her seemingly ravenous appetite for bacon.

The unaffected glimpses of her bare shoulder as the gown slipped off it, and the curve of her back seen through the gap in the back of it.

He laughed, and turned around, just in time to see her walk out the room.

If it was at all possible, she looked more beautiful in the daylight.

He gasped. Even after being admitted to hospital for a night, she took his breath away, and he did not want to let her out of his sight again.

"Just let me get my things," he said, ducking back into the room for his jacket, throwing it on and patting the pocket to make sure the wallet was there.

"Anything else?" he asked, and she shook her head shyly.

He held out his hand, and after a pause, she took it and he felt the hairs on his arm stand on end.

Her hand fit perfectly in the palm of his.

The lift was crowded, but he pulled her in close to the edge and shielded her with his body.

And soon, they were standing hand in hand, just outside the Grattan Street forecourt.

He wanted to run down the street, holding her hand, and jump into a tram as if he was in a 1950s movie, but the streams of cars and pedestrians and traffic lights forbade it.

Not to worry. She was there with him, and at least he could savour the closeness.

"So what's next?" he asked.

She swung his arm back and forth as she thought about it. "I can't go to the hotel, and I can't go home, but I've discovered I'm exhausted."

She yawned widely, and he smothered a yawn himself.

"I don't want to seem overly pushy, but if I can't take you to yours, do you want to come to mine?"

"I thought you'd never ask," she said so impishly, he laughed.

"Very well then," let's go outside and see if we can get a taxi.

She shivered in the cool morning air, so he took his jacket off and slid it around her shoulders where it was almost knees length on her. Adorably so.

Impulsively he dropped a kiss on the top of her head.

They didn't manage to get the first taxi they saw, but after a couple of attempts they were on the way.

He slipped an arm around her shoulder as they moved though the City and out the other side, stopping at his Queens Road apartment building.

He paid the driver, and gave Ava a moment to look out over Albert Park.

"I run around the lake every morning," he said.

She turned to look at him critically, "it shows."

She looked back, "your apartment must have cost a tonne of money."

"Not as much as it's worth now," he said with an ironic smile, and moved his arm to gesture towards to building.

Seemingly overawed, she clutched his hand as she moved towards the building.

The lift was swift and silent, and as usual he was grateful for that.

Perhaps even more so with Ava on board.

He opened the door, and stepped back to let her go first, grinning a little as she absorbed the panoramic view of Albert Park and Port Phillip Bay.

She walked across the Living/Dining room, opened the sliding door and walked out onto the balcony.

"How do you get anything done around here with that view?"

He lightly rested his hands on her shoulders, "it is distracting," he said, meaning her.

She snorted, seeming to understand.

"Do you want to take a shower? I can find you a t-shirt of mine to wear."

"Actually yes," she said.

Back in the apartment he found her a clean t-shirt to wear, a clean towel and unopened tablet of soap to use. He took them out to her, "care to see the facilities?"

While she showered in the guest bathroom, he showered in the ensuite.

When he emerged in track pants and a t-shirt, she was already curled up, asleep in his bed.

He folded the bedspread over the top of her, and debated about staying there, or moving to the guest room.

But stripped of make-up, she seemed younger. More innocent.

He lay next to her, closed his eyes, and drifted off.

He woke to find himself half under the covers, with Ava a warm solid presence behind him.

Her arm was wound around him, and she was stroking his leg with her foot.

It was kind of nice.

He wriggled around as he rolled over so he could see her face, trying not to hurt her injured hand.

They looked at each other for a long moment, before he leaned towards her, testing.

When she didn't draw away, he leaned a little closed and brushed her lips with his.

He widened the gap again and searched her face.

No shock or revulsion, but there was something softer about her. He couldn't say for sure what it was, but he kissed her again.

For a little longer.

She broke the kiss, and looked at him steadily, "you could have anyone."

He shrugged one shoulder, "I don't want anyone, I want you."

She laughed.

"Honestly, I can't believe I didn't know you existed yesterday. I feel like I've known you forever."

"Then shut up and kiss me."

Some time later, Ava's stomach rumbled.

"Are you hungry again already?"

She patted her stomach and grinned, "I sure am! I've been so busy in the last few days, I've hardly had time to eat! And once I've eaten, I've decisions to make."

Ryan leaned on one elbow, "you should stay here," he blurted out.

"Can I?"

He nodded.

"That would make this the best Christmas ever!"

One decision down, she flung herself on him again, and they didn't surfaced for some time.

THE END

ABOUT THE AUTHOR

Alexandria Blaelock writes stories, some of them for *Ellery Queen's Mystery Magazine* and *Pulphouse Fiction Magazine*. She's also written five self-help books applying business techniques to personal matters like getting dressed, cleaning house, and feeding your friends.

As a recovering Project Manager, she's probably too fond of sticking to plan. She lives in a forest because she enjoys birdsong, the scent of gum leaves and the sun on her face. When not telecommuting to parallel universes from her Melbourne based imagination, she watches K-dramas, talks to animals, and drinks Campari. At the same time.

Discover more at www.alexandriablaelock.com.

BOOKS BY
ALEXANDRIA BLAELOCK

SHORT STORY COLLECTIONS

The Histories of Hayward Hall
Lovelorn, Lovestruck and Love at First Sight
Common or Garden Variety Heroes
Case Files of the Wilkinson Detective Agency
Unavoidable Fates
Christmas Travesties

OTHER FICTION

That Love Nonsense

MS BLAELOCK'S BOOKS

Stress Free Dinner Parties
Signature Wardrobe Planning
Holistic Personal Finance
Minimally Viable Housekeeping
Planning a Life Worth Living

SELECTED SHORT STORIES

Alma's Grace
Balancing the Book
Carmelita Basingstoke
Fate in Your Hands
Kiss of Death
Lady of the Looking Glass
Life in the Security Directorate
Long Weekend in the Snow
Love in the Past Tense
Love in the Security Directorate
Morning Star, Evening Star, Superstar
Needy Bitch
Payton's Run
Phoenix Child
Secret Singer
Shining Star
Ship in a Bottle
Simone Says Hands in the Air
Special Relativity in Space
The Bygone Boyfriend
The Day the Schedule Broke
The Ghost Detectors
The Guardian's Vigil
The Mince Pie Mystery
The Mystery of the Master Suite
The Pseudonym's Bride
The Shadow Thieves
The Time-Space Paradox
Toy Soldiers